Floop's
Flowers

Text by Carole Tremblay
Illustrations by Steve Beshwaty

alphabet
soup

an imprint of
WINDMILL BOOKS
New York

Published in 2010 by Windmill Books, LLC
303 Park Avenue South, Suite # 1280, New York, NY 10010-3657

Adaptations to North American Edition © 2010 Windmill Books

Original title: Le bouquet de Floup
Original Publisher: Les éditions Imagine inc
© Carole Tremblay / Steve Beshwaty 2007
© Les éditions Imagine inc. 2007
English text © Les éditions Imagine inc 2007

Text by Carole Tremblay
Illustrations by Steve Beshwaty

Publisher Cataloging in Publication

Tremblay, Carole, 1959-
        Floop's flowers / text by Carole Tremblay ; illustrations by Steve Beshwaty.
p.   cm. – (Floop)
Summary: While preparing for a party for his friends, Floop gets distracted in the flower garden.
ISBN 978-1-60754-344-2 (lib.) – ISBN 978-1-60754-346-6 (pbk.)
ISBN 978-1-60754-345-9 (6-pack)
1. Parties—Juvenile fiction   2. Absent-mindedness—Juvenile fiction
3. Flowers—Juvenile fiction   4. Friendship—Juvenile fiction   [1. Parties—Fiction   2. Flowers—Fiction   3. Friendship—Fiction]   I. Beshwaty, Steve   II. Title   III. Series
        [E]—dc22

Printed in the United States of America

Floop invites his friends Little Bob, Kluck, and Cork over for a snack.

He has made them a yummy feast.

All he has to do is set the table.

First, Floop puts the tablecloth in place.

Next, he brings the plates.

His colorful glasses make the
table look pretty.

With straws, it's even better.

How about adding a vase of flowers? That would be nice, but Floop doesn't have any flowers.

10

No problem, Floop goes to the garden to pick some flowers.

Floop is happy.
He rolls around in the green grass.

He leaps over a big stone.

Oh! A butterfly lands on his nose.

Oooo, it tickles!

Floop laughs so hard the butterfly flies away.

Floop picks a flower. Mmm! It smells good!

What's that? Ants walking across a stone.

Hi, little ants!

Floop tickles them with a blade of grass.
The ants giggle.

Floop hears his friends calling.

Oh no! He only had time to pick one flower!

But that's okay . . .

. . . picking flowers with friends is even more fun!